ANTELOPE

DESPERATE DRAGONS

by

ANDREW WHITEHEAD

Illustrated by Rowan Clifford

HAMISH HAMILTON
LONDON

For my nephews,
Jamie and Lewis

HAMISH HAMILTON LTD

Published by the Penguin Group
27 Wrights Lane, London w8 5tz, England
Penguin Books USA Inc., 375 Hudson Street, New York, New York 10014, USA
Penguin Books Australia Ltd, Ringwood, Victoria, Australia
Penguin Books Canada Ltd, 2801 John Street, Markham, Ontario, Canada l3r 1b4
Penguin Books (NZ) Ltd, 182–190 Wairau Road, Auckland 10, New Zealand

Penguin Books Ltd, Registered Offices: Harmondsworth, Middlesex, England

First published in Great Britain 1991 by Hamish Hamilton Ltd

Text copyright © 1991 by Andrew Whitehead
Illustrations copyright © 1991 by Rowan Clifford

1 3 5 7 9 10 8 6 4 2

A CIP catalogue record for this book is available from the British Library

isbn 0-241-13094-8

Set in 15pt Baskerville by Rowland Phototypesetting Ltd
Bury St Edmunds, Suffolk
Reproduced, printed and bound in Great Britain by
BPCC Hazell Books, Aylesbury, Bucks, Member of BPCC Ltd.

1. Dragons Prancing

IT HAD BEEN months since any of the dragons had caught a maid and held her for ransom in their caves atop Singed Spruce Mountain. Life had become one long holiday of eating and lounging about in the sun. But idleness was beginning to catch up with them, and, for the past week, Beaconbreath had been pacing around anxiously . . .

"We've been getting lazy," he said gloomily. "Lazy. And broke. We're down to our last five crowns. We

1

'aven't kidnapped a maid in ages."

"'Ang on, didn't I bring one back the other day?" said Heathaze dreamily. "A little one, with a wooden 'andle. That was it, a maid."

"A *maid*! A *maid*! That was a SPADE!" Beaconbreath roared. "See, you've even forgotten what they look like now!"

"Mmm, I thought it didn't put up much of a struggle."

"Well, it wouldn't, would it? Spades aren't so fussy about bein' snatched and held for ransom, and then bein' rescued by knights in shinin' armour! A couple of days in one of our caves – it's like an 'oliday to them, isn't it? They can get their feet up for a bit – get away from all that diggin' and stuff!"

"Yeah, but they don't make much noise, though," added Furnaceface.

"What you on about?" snorted Beaconbreath, turning on his friend furiously.

"Well, they give you a right 'eadache, don't they, them maids? All that shoutin' and screamin', and kickin' your kneecaps, and pokin' you up the nostrils with those long

3

fingernails. I think we should change over to spades."

"Or wheelbarrows!" suggested Heathaze, with sudden inspiration. "It'd save all that carryin'. And if we snatched spades as well, we could put the spades *in* the wheelbarrows!"

"Ooooh, that's a good idea!" cried Furnaceface, and he grinned broadly.

Beaconbreath gaped at his two friends, bewildered.

"I don't believe this!" he said. "We're supposed to be runnin' a dragonery up 'ere – not a garden centre! And we 'aven't 'ad a damsel in distress for ages!"

"Yeah, well not to worry, eh?" said Heathaze jauntily. "Anyone fancy rollin' some rocks on a few peasants?"

Beaconbreath was far from amused;

he glowered and pointed to a rock beside his cave.

"Try that one," he said mysteriously.

"What, your rock?" replied Heathaze, puzzled.

"Yes, go on, take it."

"Ooh, I don't know. I mean, it's *your* rock, Beaconbreath. *Your* rock."

"Oh, I don't mind," coaxed Beaconbreath. "Just this once." And he started to smirk.

"Welllll . . ."

At first Heathaze was reluctant to take the rock for a missile. It was Beaconbreath's pride and joy; the one on which he always counted his loot. But after a few minutes' consideration – well, it was such a useful sort of rock, and the perfect size for peasant-squashing – he knew he had to

6

have it, and he nudged it gingerly with his snout.

It was at that moment that a small buff-coloured envelope revealed itself to him.

In the top left-hand corner of the envelope were the words *Collector of Taxes*.

Heathaze cringed with fear.

"W-what is it?" he stammered.

"It came last week," Beaconbreath announced. "You might as well know, lads. The Tax Gatherers are on to us. You know how everyone's supposed to send money for things like new schools and libraries, and we never do? They've had an undercover investigator on our case. They say we owe ten thousand crowns – and it's due next week!"

Furnaceface's jaw dropped open and Heathaze started whimpering.

"But we 'aven't got ten thousand crowns."

"I know! I know!" exclaimed Beaconbreath. "Because we 'aven't snatched any damsels in ages!"

"Oooooh, what are we going to do?"

"Well, don't look at me! It's your fault!" Beaconbreath growled, pointing an accusatory claw at his two companions.

"*Our* fault!" Heathaze and Furnaceface cried in unison.

"Well, whose idea was it to do a bit of mini-cab driving the other month when we got a bit skint? You two! That's how they found out about us! That's why they've been checking up on us! Yesss, I've been thinking. Remember that young girl we used to drive to the village hall, the one who teaches aerobics. . . ?"

"Bonnie Bendybits?"

"That's the one. It was probably her, this *undercover investigator*. Yesss . . . too nice by far. I always thought that. I bet *she's* the one who's got it in for us. Yesss . . ."

Heathaze and Furnaceface were now quivering with fear.

"Ooooh, what are we going to do, Beaconbreath?" they whined.

"Don't worry, lads! We'll be all right! I've got a plan!" announced

Beaconbreath, and he started chuckling wildly. "How do you fancy doing a spot of keep-fit?"

Down in the village, the people looked across the fields to Singed Spruce Mountain. Some of the village folk thought they could hear it thundering up there, but the older, and wiser, ones knew it was three desperate dragons laughing maniacally.

2. *Ladies Dancing*

"ONE, TWO! ONE, two!" said Bonnie
Bendybits to the Ladies of the Court.

"Three, four! Three, four!" returned
the Ladies of the Court to Bonnie
Bendybits.

"And . . . STOP!" cried Bonnie
Bendybits as she took the gramophone
needle off a recording of *Work Out with
William Walton*. "Take a breather and
then we'll do half an hour to *Party Hot
Hits of Handel and Haydn*."

From the ranks of maids and

courtiers stepped forth the pretty daughter of King Octavius.

"Am I doing all right?" she said.

"You're coming along excellently, Princess Faustina," said Bonnie Bendybits. "In fact, because you're doing so well, and because I've been short of staff recently, I was going to ask you if you'd be good enough to take the next session."

"I'd love to!" said Princess Faustina. "And you're certainly right about exercising. It makes one feel so full of life and energy. And so happy too. I know this is going to be a very special day."

3. Dragons Scheming

BY NOW THE dragons were plodding determinedly down their mountain track on their way to the village. As usual, Beaconbreath took the lead, his nostrils occasionally twitching and giving out little plumes of smoke as he savoured the task ahead.

The plan was simple. They would snatch Bonnie Bendybits and hold her for ransom for the sum of ten thousand crowns. Anxious to get their ace investigator back, the Tax Gatherers

14

would send the money immediately, and the dragons would be able to pay back the ten thousand crowns as the amount they owed in taxes.

Only one thing worried them, and that was how to constrain Bonnie Bendybits when the snatch was made. It was a long trek back to Singed Spruce Mountain and there was a chance she might escape. But that problem would have to wait.

On entering Mysterious Wood, the dragons were still in high spirits. But when the trees became dense, and gloom surrounded them, they were soon forced to stop and check their bearings.

"'Ere, Beaconbreath," enquired Heathaze, "are you sure we're goin' the right way through this wood?"

"'Course I'm sure," Beaconbreath replied uncertainly.

"Yeah, well, I know about these Mysterious Wood things. I read this book once about two kids called Hansel and Kettle, who meet this wolf choppin' down a beanstalk called Little Red Robin Hood . . . I tell you, after that, give me Beatrix Potter any day . . ."

"Ssshh!" interrupted Beaconbreath. "What was that?"

The three dragons pricked up their ears to a sound that chilled Heathaze to the bone. It was the CHOP! CHOP! CHOP! of a woodcutter's axe.

"Blimey! It's 'im!" said Heathaze trembling. "It's Little Red Robin Hood. I'm gettin' out of 'ere!"

But before Heathaze could move a muscle, a human was addressing them from the direction of the chopping.

"Welcome to Mysterious Wood. I'm Tom Oakstaff!"

"Name ring a bell?" Beaconbreath whispered to Heathaze out of the corner of his mouth.

"It's all right. We're safe," Heathaze said, sighing. "I think he was the good guy in *Hansel and Kettle*."

Tom Oakstaff approached them.

18

"And what are *you* doing in Mysterious Wood, my friends?" he said.

"Er . . . we're . . . er . . . on our way to kidna . . . I mean, join the Bonnie Bendybits aerobics class," said Beaconbreath.

"Then take a luncheon with me before you continue your journey," said Tom Oakstaff.

"Yes, well, that's . . . er . . . very kind of you, Mr Elmtwig . . ." Beaconbreath began awkwardly, "but . . ."

"It's *Oakstaff*," Tom corrected.

"Oh, yes. Sorry, but we're . . . er . . . in a bit of a hurry, you know. Must get fighting the old flab. Perhaps next time, Mr Beechbranch."

Tom looked dismayed.

"Ah well," he shrugged. "Never

mind . . . but if I can ever be of service to you . . ."

"No, no, I don't think so. You see . . ." Then an idea suddenly struck Beaconbreath and his eyes twinkled with delight. "You say you're a *woodcutter*?"

"The best in these parts," said Tom Oakstaff, with an embarrassed little cough.

"What, and you . . . er . . . make *things* with wood too, do you?"

"You name it. Chairs, tables, doors, windows . . ."

"Er, boxes?" Beaconbreath enquired, trying not to sound too interested.

"Why, yes. I could make you a fine box," said Tom Oakstaff. "But . . ."

Beaconbreath's mind whirled frantically and then a grin spread slowly across his face. He knew his plan was complete. With a voice full of authority, he turned to Furnaceface and said, "Furnaceface, give Tom Treetrunk 'ere the five crowns. 'E's going to make us a box!"

Within half an hour the little

wooden box was finished. Furnaceface handed over their last five crowns; Beaconbreath praised Tom Larchleaf's craftsmanship, and the three dragons set off with renewed vigour through Mysterious Wood.

Nothing was to dampen their spirits. Once or twice they had the feeling they were being followed, but they knew deer were numerous and often moved around unseen in the forest.

4. *Ladies Screaming*

BONNIE BENDYBITS REPLACED the needle on the record and the aerobics session started again.

"One, two! One, two!" said Princess Faustina to the Ladies of the Court.

"Three, four! Three, four!" returned the Ladies of the Court to Princess Faustina.

"Smash the door! Smash the door!" cried Beaconbreath to Furnaceface and Heathaze.

"In we go! In we go!" shouted the

dragons as the door was wrenched from its hinges and flung across the room.

"AAAGHH! DRAGONS!!!" screamed the Ladies of the Court when the trio burst into the hall.

At once the scene became a mass of flailing arms and claws. Heathaze was booted on the kneecaps and for a time was put out of commission. Furnaceface spent the first minute of the snatch trying to dislodge a long-nailed finger from up his left nostril. Only Beaconbreath managed to stave off the advancing hordes of Ladies of the Court.

"Open the box!" he bellowed to his friends.

Fending off blows from all around him, Furnaceface managed to open the box.

"It's done!" he cried.

"Now, grab Bonnie Bendybits!" Beaconbreath commanded.

"Got her!" cried Furnaceface, as he was punched in the ribs by a bony fist.

"Er . . . excuse me, madam . . ." said Heathaze politely, to a rather vicious Lady of the Court, "is it really necessary to keep kicking me on the kneecaps?"

"Oh, awfully sorry," said the Lady of the Court, and she kicked him on the shins instead.

"Get the lid on!" cried Beaconbreath, as he fought off an attack from their left flank.

"She's in!" exclaimed Furnaceface, as he caught a second blow that made him double up in pain.

"Right! A final effort now, lads!
Now, PUSH!!!"

Gradually, the three dragons
managed to force the Ladies of the
Court to a room at the back of the hall.
When the last arms and legs had been
pushed and prodded out of sight,
Beaconbreath closed the door on the
Ladies of the Court and ran the two

securing bolts home with his teeth.

The snatch was a success! Bonnie Bendybits was in the bag – well, box – and the first part of the operation was over.

The trio quickly slipped back into Mysterious Wood and followed the forest path towards Singed Spruce Mountain. Nothing marred their hearty retreat; they knew ten thousand crowns was within their grasp. And though they occasionally caught sight of watching eyes, they felt sure these now must be timid deer.

5. *Tom is Helping*

BUT HELP WAS soon at hand in the village hall.

"Let us go! Let us go!" cried the Ladies of the Court.

"Half a mo! Half a mo!" said a voice in quick retort.

Strong, nimble fingers quickly drew back the door bolts and released the grateful Ladies of the Court.

"We were attacked – by DRAGONS!" they said.

"Yes, I knew they were up to no

good when I came across them in Mysterious Wood," said their rescuer comfortingly.

"What do you know about dragons?" asked the Ladies of the Court. "Who are you?"

"I'm Tom Oakstaff," said Tom Oakstaff. "I followed them at a distance through Mysterious Wood, but lost them half a mile from the village."

"They've got Bonnie Bendybits," said a sobbing Lady of the Court.

"Ah, that's what *you* think!" said a voice from behind the gramophone. And up popped Bonnie Bendybits. "I hid here when I realised they were trying to kidnap me."

"Well, if *you're* not in the box," everyone chorused "then *who* is?"

6. Dragons Yelping

DOWN IN THE village, the people looked
across the fields to Singed Spruce
Mountain. Some of the village folk
thought they could hear it thundering
up there, but the older, and wiser, ones
knew it was three desperate dragons
rejoicing uproariously.

"We 'aven't lost the old touch, 'ave
we, eh, boys?" said Beaconbreath,
laughing.

"Pity we didn't 'ave a bigger box!"
roared Furnaceface. "We could've
snatched the lot of 'em!"

"My kneecaps aren't 'alf smartin'," whined Heathaze.

The dragons stared at the prize before them and beamed victoriously.

"Now for the ransom note," Beaconbreath hissed sneakily.

"Yesss, the ransom note," the other two dragons hissed with equal glee.

Taking a large block of slate and a great hunk of chalk, Beaconbreath quickly scrawled away at the ransom note.

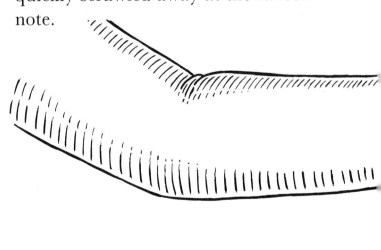

WE AS THE
BENDIBITTS WE IS
RANSUMMING ER FOR
MUNNY. SEND TEN THOUSAND
CROWNSE TO SINJ SPRUUS
MOUNTAIN BY SUNNUP.
WE MEENZ BIZNISS SO
DON'T MUKK US ABOUT
OR YULE BE INFERRIT.
ANONIMUSSLY,
BEEKUNBRETH.

"Perfect!" said Beaconbreath, signing his name with a flourish.

"Er, excuse me, but I think you may have a little problem," came a muffled voice from within the box.

"Oh, you do, do you?" growled Beaconbreath.

"Yes," the voice replied.

Beaconbreath sniffed contemptuously.

"Us dragons don't know the meaning of the word 'problem'!" he said.

"You will when you take the lid off the box," said the petulant voice.

The dragons looked at each other in consternation. Had they overlooked something? Had their perfect plan an unseen flaw?

Beaconbreath quickly removed the lid from the box and peered inside.

Instantly, all the parts of his body that had previously been up suddenly went down: his jaw dropped, his heart sank, and his eyelids lowered.

"I wonder which bit comes off first when they hang, draw and quarter you," he said.

"What you on about?" said Furnaceface.

"Lads," said Beaconbreath, with an incredulous grimace, "we've gone and snatched Princess Faustina!"

7.   *Reaper Jeering*

IN THE ROYAL Apartments of the castle, the King was questioning everyone.

"Now then, you say my daughter has been taken by dragons?"

"Yes," said Bonnie Bendybits, anxious to be of assistance.

"But can you give me a description?"

"Well, she's sort of small and fair and wearing a red leotard."

"Yes, I know what my daughter

looks like," the King said patiently. "I meant the *dragons*."

"Oh yes . . . well, er . . . *dragons*, I suppose," said Bonnie Bendybits, puzzled.

The King sighed and shook his head in bewildered disbelief.

"Remind me not to make you Chief of Police," he said.

Pushing past the Ladies of the Court, Tom Oakstaff stepped forward to console his monarch.

"I don't think your daughter will come to any harm, Your Majesty," he said. "These dragons may be bad, but they're certainly not cruel. And it appears it was a genuine mistake."

"That may be so, Mr Oakstaff," the King replied regally, "but Faustina is my only daughter and everything possible must be done to secure her

safe release. No, I fear serious measures must be taken. Dragon Reaper must be sent for."

"Not *Dragon Reaper*!" squealed the Ladies of the Court.

"Yes, Dragon Reaper!" repeated the King.

Tom and Bonnie gasped in horror too. It was so unfair. Dragon Reaper was the most ruthless fighter of dragons in the land. No creature was safe from his silver lance. No animal stood a chance against the

awesome power of Silver Reaper.

But the King's mind was made up, and he was already turning to one of his footmen.

"I must get in touch with him at once," he said. "Bring me the Yellow Pages."

Without delay, five young boys dressed in primrose tunics were sent for and instructed to scour every tavern for Dragon Reaper. Within half an hour, the doors to the Royal Apartments were thrown open and in strode the tall, black-hearted figure of **DRAGON REAPER!**

He eyed the gathering grimly, and swaggered towards the King with evil intent.

"So," he sneered, "you wish to pay for the services of Dragon Reaper?"

"It would appear I have no choice,"

the King said sadly. "By now these creatures will know they have the wrong victim and may be provoked to harm my daughter. Name your price, Dragon Reaper."

The evil knight's eyes fell greedily upon the monarch's sceptre.

"Why, that's easy," he said. "The Palace, all your lands and . . . the Royal Throne."

"NEVER!" cried the Ladies of the Court.

"Wait!" exclaimed the King.

He was wretched. He slumped into a chair looking wan and sickly, but he nodded his assent.

"Very well. I agree. The loss of my Kingdom is a small price to pay for the safe return of my daughter. Bring her safely home, Dragon Reaper, and everything I have will be yours."

"Then we have a deal," said Dragon Reaper, and he smirked as he watched the Ladies of the Court flood the Royal Apartments with their bitter tears.

It was during this time that Tom Oakstaff grabbed Bonnie Bendybits by the hand and said, "Come on, Bonnie, we've got work to do."

Leaving by the servants' staircase, they made their way across the courtyard and headed for Mysterious Wood.

"There's still time to save the day," said Tom, as he stopped to blow his hunting horn.

"What *are* you doing?" said Bonnie Bendybits.

"Wait and see," said Tom mysteriously.

Suddenly, from behind trees and

45

bushes, bird noises answered the call of the hunting horn, and Tom smiled contentedly as he put his plan into operation.

8. Dragons Fearing

MEANWHILE, BACK ON Singed Spruce
Mountain, Beaconbreath was looking
desperate.

"Well, that's it, then. Anybody got
any particular choice about the cliff we
should throw ourselves off?"

"We could starve ourselves to
death," suggested Heathaze.

"Yes, yes, true. And there's
drownin' and poisonin', and beatin'
each other over the 'ead with rocks and
logs."

47

"What if I made a nice hemlock trifle?" said Heathaze.

"Yes, yes, that too has possibilities – especially as I'm still suffering from the raspberry one you made last week . . ."

Princess Faustina stifled a laugh and turned away from the doleful trio.

"I suppose you find all this very funny," said Beaconbreath, smarting.

"Well, you *are* rather silly," laughed Princess Faustina. "I wouldn't let my father hurt you, even though it was wrong of you to do what you did. Though I am interested to know *why* you wanted to kidnap Bonnie Bendybits in the first place."

Beaconbreath poured out his sorrowful tale about Bonnie Bendybits and the Tax Gatherers, the ten thousand crowns they owed, and the plan he had devised to get it.

"What a silly idea!" exclaimed Princess Faustina. "And you really thought you could get away with it?"

"Yes," the three dragons whimpered.

"Really! I think I'd better get back at once, to sort out this little mess."

"Er, if you wouldn't mind," the dragons snivelled.

"Come on, lead the way."

The three dragons set off, leading Princess Faustina along their mountain track. Their plan had been very foolish – they could see this now – and it was lucky it had been Princess Faustina they had snatched and not Bonnie Bendybits. But as they reached a position below their caves, a sight met them that robbed them of their rekindled spirits, stopped them dead in

their tracks, and turned them into the palest shade of green they had ever been in their lives.

There in the distance, far across Mysterious Wood, was the castle of King Octavius, and flying proudly from the battlements was the standard of *Dragon Reaper*!

"DRAGON REAPER!!!" the dragons shrieked.

Princess Faustina was dismayed too.

"My goodness!" she cried. "Now I really do fear you are in trouble. I think we could be too late."

The dragons cowered and trembled.

Then a voice shouted, "Hellowww . . ."

"It's 'im," said Beaconbreath, panicking, as he tried to hide behind Princess Faustina. "Dragon Reaper! 'E's come to get us!"

"Now he's hardly likely to come announcing his arrival," said the exasperated Princess.

"Eh? Oh no. Per'aps you're right. Yes. Silly me. Never thought of that. Who can it be, then?"

As the lone figure came into sight from behind a large boulder, the dragons sighed with relief as a man's features became more recognisable.

"It's Fred 'Ollybush!" Beaconbreath cried. "Fred 'Ollybush! The bloke what made us the box! Watcha, Fred!"

"It's *Tom*," Tom Oakstaff said testily. "TOM! And I'm not a *Hollybush*, I'm an *Oakstaff*!"

"Yes, well, never mind what you are, mate. I'd rather 'ave you up 'ere than old Dragon Reaper."

Sighing, and shaking his head sadly, Tom turned round and pointed to a cloud of dust beyond Mysterious Wood. "See that dust cloud?" he said. "*There* is your Dragon Reaper."

The dragons' jaws dropped open and they began to shake uncontrollably. Dragon Reaper was on the road that led to Mysterious Wood and within half an hour he would be upon them.

"You have just one chance," announced Tom Oakstaff.

"We'll take it!" cried the dragons.

"I haven't told you what it is yet."

"It doesn't matter. We'll do it, we'll do it!"

And so Tom Oakstaff explained his plan to defeat Dragon Reaper, as Bonnie Bendybits tried her best to waylay the wicked knight in Mysterious Wood.

Tom began. "The King has given his word that he will hand over his lands when Princess Faustina is returned. Even now the evil Reaper will be drooling at the thought of the riches that will soon be his . . ."

" 'E's no mug, is 'e?" said Beaconbreath.

"Even though it appears you are prepared to escort Princess Faustina back to her father, I foresee Dragon Reaper will still wish to slay you and

56

take her back himself for the wealth that awaits . . ." continued Tom.

"A man after me own heart," mused Beaconbreath. "Now then," he said to Tom Oakstaff, "getting back to this 'just one chance' business. You know, the *get-out* clause . . ?"

"Ah yes," continued Tom Oakstaff. "You and I will challenge Dragon Reaper when he reaches the foothills of Singed Spruce Mountain. I have my trusty axe and I feel that . . ."

"Er, just a minute, Mr Pineplank," Beaconbreath interrupted. "All this romantic stuff, you know, about challenging Dragon Reaper – just 'ow much time do you spend in the forest? That silver lance thing 'e's got, it's not a toothpick, you know! One prod with that and my kidneys could be seein' daylight! No, I'm sorry, you're on the

wrong mountain. You want the
Fearless, Brave and Dashing Dragon.
I'm the Sissy, Soft and Cowardly
variety."

It was at this moment that Beaconbreath noticed all eyes were upon him, imploring him to do what a dragon – especially a *desperate* dragon – sometimes has to do. He would have to face Dragon Reaper with Tom Whateverhisnamewas, no matter how slim their chances. The evil knight was entering Mysterious Wood now and he would be with them before they had a chance to escape. It seemed there was no alternative.

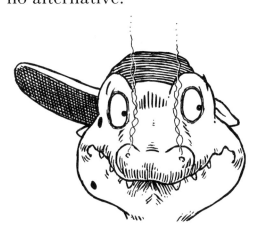

Smiling bravely at his two companions, Beaconbreath sniffed the air in a dramatic and heroic manner as, he had heard, all great warriors did before going into battle, saying, "Well, lads, this is it, then. But if anythin' goes wrong . . ."

"Name it, Beaconbreath," Furnaceface said. "Name it."

"Every twelfth of May, roll some rocks on a few peasants to remember me by."

"I promise," said Furnaceface. "I promise."

In an effort to raise Beaconbreath's flagging spirits, Tom held aloft his leather satchel and said, "Don't worry, Beaconbreath, we still have this."

"Eh? Oh yes, wonderful," sighed Beaconbreath. "Five thousand knights in the land and I get the one with the 'andbag."

"No, you don't understand," said Tom. "I'm a . . ."

But his speech was cut short by the call of a hunting horn from Mysterious Wood, and before Beaconbreath knew what was happening, Tom Oakstaff was leaping on his back and riding him down the mountain track.

9. *Reaper Lancing*

IT WAS ON a barren stretch of land that Beaconbreath and Tom Oakstaff waited for Dragon Reaper. A chill wind blew across the foothills, and the animals of Mysterious Wood sat in rows along the branches of the trees waiting for the big punch-up.

Beaconbreath was trembling so much that Tom Oakstaff was in serious danger of being jiggled off his back.

"There's no need to be nervous," Tom said gently.

"Oh, I'm not nervous," replied Beaconbreath. "I just have this allergy to fear."

"Just remember. I have my trusty axe!"

"Oh yes. And your trusty 'andbag. Don't forget that. Per'aps we should use that first . . . you know . . . and get 'im in a good mood."

"Sshh!" Tom said. "Dragon Reaper approaches."

Dressed in black armour, astride an equally black charger, Dragon Reaper rode from the gloom of Mysterious Wood. In his hand was Silver Reaper, the most feared weapon known to dragons. No animal had survived a blow from this powerful lance; and as Beaconbreath gazed upon its frightening majesty, he began wondering if marshmallows felt like he

did now, when they were popped on
forks and toasted in front of open
fires.

"You don't think a little apology
might, er . . ." he said.

"Quiet, Beaconbreath," said Tom.
"Prepare yourself."

"I wonder what I'll look like as
three hundred pairs of men's shoes,"

whimpered Beaconbreath. "You don't think . . ."

"Quiet!" said Tom. "He comes."

Dragon Reaper was kicking on his charger now and galloping towards Beaconbreath and Tom Oakstaff.

"On!" cried Dragon Reaper.

"On!" cried Tom Oakstaff.

But Beaconbreath was frozen to the spot, transfixed by the dazzling lance Dragon Reaper was pointing directly at his heart.

"On!" repeated Tom Oakstaff, digging his heels hard into Beaconbreath's ribs.

But Tom's spurring had no effect; Beaconbreath stood his ground – and trembled. And as he trembled, he began to jiggle Tom Oakstaff up and down his back, forcing his companion

to let loose his axe in order to maintain his balance.

THWACK! It landed on Beaconbreath's foot and he cried out in pain. "Ohhh! Me toe!"

Up reared Dragon Reaper's horse in fright, not understanding why a dragon should cry out *before* it had been pierced by Silver Reaper!

And then out of the saddle shot Dragon Reaper, launched like a rocket when the horse began to buck!

He landed with a CLANG! beside the now unseated Tom Oakstaff, dazed but grinning wildly as he saw the woodcutter was unarmed.

"You'll do first," he said to Tom, and he drew his sword from its scabbard. "Say farewell to the world, woodcutter. Then I'll finish off these dragons. They'll be my tenth victims this year."

But as Dragon Reaper raised his sword high above Tom Oakstaff's head, Tom reached for his leather satchel and said, "Wait! That's proof enough!"

"Wait? For what?" Dragon Reaper cried.

"Dragon Reaper," said Tom, taking a large buff-coloured envelope from his satchel and handing it to the evil knight, "read this!"

Even before he had opened it
Dragon Reaper was already shaking in
his armour, for in the top left-hand
corner of the envelope were the words
Collector of Taxes.

"I'm Tom Oakstaff!" Tom revealed.
"Undercover Investigator with the
Tax Gatherers. I'm arresting you for
trading as a dragon slayer and refusing
to pay your taxes. Grab him, lads!"

Instantly, four men ran into the clearing and grappled Dragon Reaper to the floor. They were Tom's colleagues. They were covered in a camouflage of leaves and sticks and each had a bird whistle around his neck.

"Now I understand!" exclaimed Bonnie Bendybits. "These are the

feathered friends who answered the call of your hunting horn! Fine friends indeed!''

''It's the best way to keep in touch,'' explained Tom, smiling. ''It saves a fortune in postage stamps.''

Even the evil Dragon Reaper was too shocked to struggle. With a human tree at each leg and arm, he was marched away to the Department of Tax Gatherers for further interrogation.

''There, I said I had something up my sleeve,'' said Tom. ''Didn't I, Beaconbreath? Beaconbreath . . ?''

But Beaconbreath was slinking away towards Mysterious Wood, mindful of Tom being the Undercover Investigator.

''Er, just a minute, Beaconbreath!'' Tom commanded. ''I want a word with you!''

"And me too!" said Bonnie Bendybits, and she stepped from the gloom of Mysterious Wood to obstruct Beaconbreath's path.

"Er, I was just off to tell the King everything was all right," said Beaconbreath breezily.

"Were you now?" Tom said.

"Er, yes. Clever of me to, er, shout out, like, and frighten his horse, wasn't it? Deserve a medal, I suppose. Kind of thing a hero does, isn't it? Eh? Yes. Mind you, I don't ask for thanks – oh, no – we've always been brave, us . . ."

But Tom and Bonnie seemed less than convinced of Beaconbreath's bravery – and sincerity; they only regarded him dourly when he preened and grinned.

"Er, I sent you a letter recently," Tom began.

"Oh yes!" exclaimed Beaconbreath. "We'd love to come to your birthday party! We like a bit of jelly, and cakes, and . . ."

"You know what I mean," said Tom grimly. "Tax!"

TAX! There was that word again! It made Beaconbreath shudder visibly. It was like BATH! or BRUSH YOUR TEETH! or NO, YOU'RE NOT GOING OUT UNTIL YOU'VE TIDIED YOUR ROOM!

Beaconbreath started to whimper.

But Tom and Bonnie weren't heartless, and Princess Faustina was quick to support the hapless trio, too.

"They only wanted to pay their taxes," she said. "Don't be hard on them. I'm sure we could think of something, couldn't we? So they might *earn* some money?"

"Could we . . . ? said Tom, to Bonnie Bendybits.

"Welllll . . ." mused Bonnie, smiling, "there is *one* thing I have in mind . . ."

10. *Dragons Dancing*

"ONE, TWO! ONE, two!" said three dragons to the Ladies of the Court.

"Three, four! Three, four!" returned the Ladies of the Court to Beaconbreath, Heathaze and Furnaceface.

"This is a bore! And me leotard's tore!" said Beaconbreath, ungrammatically, to the Ladies of the Court.

"Then you'd better move slower! And get up off the floor!" returned

85

Bonnie Bendybits, laughing, at her three new, but overweight, assistants.

And so, for the first time in their lives, the three dragons became honestly employed as teachers of aerobics, paying their taxes like all good citizens. They worked hard, too. So hard in fact, that, towards the end of each day . . .

. . . Down in the village, the people looked across the fields to Singed Spruce Mountain. Some of the village folk thought they could hear it thundering up there, but the older, and wiser, ones knew it was three desperate dragons groaning – painfully!